Chapter One

The hotel clerk hands the key card to me with a smile perfected from years of practice. A short line of people waits behind me to check into their rooms. Three people chat excitedly as if they haven't seen each other in quite some time, but the man accompanying the chattiest woman has distracted himself with his phone. He's uninterested in her conversation, but remains facing them to not seem rude.

This is my first time attending the Ignited by Books Author Event in Toronto. There's a Facebook group dedicated to this community of authors, and I've tried to be present, but my social media skills lack, to say the least.

Keeping up with the latest and greatest new app gives me anxiety, and I detest promoting myself. My books are great, at least, that's what the reviews claim, but my sales aren't enough to sustain my writing career.

There are several reasons I've never attended an event. There's the cost of a table plus the inventory, swag, hotel room, and dining out. My ex-husband took care of our finances. I was told it was too far out of our budget and not feasible, so I let each one come and go.

I say ex because he left me for a younger, prettier version eleven months and twenty-two days ago. She's twenty-four; thirteen years younger than me. Life hasn't yet beaten that peppy smile off her face, but it will.

There was a time when I was happy. Seems like a lifetime ago. Greg leaving me has been an adjustment, but I'm managing. My job as an orderly at the Metro hospital earns enough money to pay the bills with some to spare.

After the divorce, I took over the house and all the financials associated with it. It wasn't nearly as expensive as he'd led on, so I questioned where *his* money went. He laughed as he confessed how he'd stowed away what he could in a secret account for two years while he planned to leave me.

I felt like a fool when he boasted about how easy it was to hide the $73,000 from my lawyer. He was so cocky about not having to give me half, while I had to buy him out of the mortgage.

I wanted to push him in front of a bus. I'm still furious, but trying to let it go. Although, if the bus opportunity comes by, I can't promise anything.

Being single after twelve years of marriage isn't all bad. When I come home from work, my house is just as clean as when I left it. He didn't leave crumbs on my sofa, muddy boot prints on

A DOMINANT'S FAVOUR
By PEBBLES LACASSE

Originally Featured in
***Ignited by Hope*:**
A Charity Anthology
created for the
Ignited by Books Author Event 2025
in Toronto, Ontario, Canada

©A DOMINANT'S FAVOUR: AN AUTHOR GAINS STRENGTH THROUGH SUBMISSION
BY PEBBLES LACASSE

THIS BOOK IS TO BE SOLD TO ADULT AUDIENCES ONLY. IT CONTAINS ADULT SITUATIONS, EXPLICIT SEXUAL SCENES AND GRAPHIC LANGUAGE, WHICH MAY BE OFFENSIVE TO SOME READERS.

ORIGINALLY PUBLISHED: IGNITED BY HOPE CHARITY ANTHOLOGY
PUBLISHED VIA PEBBLES LACASSE: JANUARY 2026
Paperback 978-1-989979-66-2

PUBLISHED BY PEBBLES LACASSE
www.pebbleslacasse.com

my freshly washed floors, and I don't have to pick wet towels off the bed.

If I don't feel like cooking dinner, I eat cereal—something forbidden when Axel lived with me. He insisted on having a solid meal for dinner every night, which meant I had to cook no matter how exhausted I was from a ten-hour shift at the hospital. Not once did he pick up a spatula. The man could barely make toast and would likely have burned down the house if he had to use the stove.

Good riddance!

The key card unlocks the door to room 527. Inside is one queen bed with a pale blue bedspread bearing tiny yellow flowers. Photos hung on the pale-yellow painted walls are basic and uninteresting. Does every room have the same prints?

My hand slides up the wall inside the bathroom until the switch flips, making me squint from the sudden blast of light. Note to self: Don't turn on the light during the night or my retinas may never recover.

At least the room is clean to the eye. No chance in hell would I use one of those lights to detect DNA. I'd never get into the bed or walk on the carpet. Sit on the fabric chair? Hell no! Absence of knowledge and all that.

With the wagon carrying everything needed for the weekend tucked in the corner, I play reverse Tetris to unpack what I won't need downstairs. My small suitcase and my computer bag took some doing to dislodge since I tucked them in to keep them from falling out.

With One hand pressed to the cool glass, I stare out the window, consciously breathing as slowly as possible. This growing panic attack will ease—they always do.

Knowing I'll be doing this venture solo is terrifying. What if I do something stupid in front of the seasoned authors? How humiliating will it be if nobody comes to my table? Will the other authors approach or leer in confusion as to why someone as small as me would bother to attend?

My palm presses to my chest, hoping that'll stop my heart from its attempt to break free of my ribs.

Inhale.

Exhale.

Just breathe.

Once the dizziness subsides, I flop on my back on the bed and arrange two pillows beneath my shoulders to prop me up. My finger skims along my phone's screen to display the group chat.

For the tenth time today, I check to ensure nothing has changed in the schedule. I'm supposed to be downstairs in the lounge for the meet-and-greet at five o'clock. That leaves me two hours to burn.

I hung my shirts to prevent wrinkles, my folded pants are in the dresser, and my make-up and hair products rest on the bathroom counter ready to go.

My fingers go wild on my keyboard as the plot to my story plays out. This is the third book in my latest romantic suspense series, and the best one yet.

Serenity from being on a higher floor outweighs the burden of my impatience while waiting for the elevator during a busy time of the day. Sound drowns in the wind before reaching the fifth-floor room, thus erasing blaring sirens, perpetual honking horns, rumbling mufflers from passing motorists, and—at my house in the cul-de-sac—the burdens of neighbours blasting ear-splitting music. But here, now, the silence allows me to drown in the story.

My fingers pause when a character's name evades me, and I glance at the clock.

Shit! Shit! Shit! I'm supposed to be downstairs in half an hour.

A sudden blast of adrenaline has me rushing off the bed, sending my computer sailing. In my haste to grab it, I trip over a box of books and land on my ass against the dresser with a loud bang.

Ouch! I'll feel that later! There's no time to complain!

I race to the bathroom and grumble at the wide eyes blinking above purple circles and blotchy skin.

Panic! No, there's no time for a panic attack! I must fight the will to cry. Deep breaths calm my racing heart and the dizzying nausea subsides.

With my hair piled atop my head, I take the fastest shower known to woman. Squeezing into the snug black jeans that make my ass look decent is a hell of a battle with damp legs! I'm panting by the time they're zipped.

My bra pushes my C-cup breasts up to where they were when I was fourteen. A sleeveless, black sequined blouse covers nicely while leaving just enough cleavage to be sexy but not tacky. The shirt is casual yet fancy while offering room for my paunchy tummy to hide from judgement. It's a physical flaw that's haunted my form from the moment I understood the pains of societal judgement.

Full-length mirrors never do my ego any favours, and yet, I stare scrutinizingly at my form.

My finger aims at the reflection of an angry woman. "No! You are beautiful, smart, and an amazing author. Your smile is strong and you're poised enough that people love you. Now shut the fuck up and let's do this!"

My nod is purposeful before I return to the bathroom.

I've outlined my hazel eyes with kohl liner, curled my lashes before dousing them in mascara, and brushed a smudge of grey shadow on my upper lids to emphasize the green hues in my eyes. A touch of translucent powder and a dab of blush to define my cheeks completes me.

I despise lipstick. No matter the brand promising no goop, my lips always feel gross. Besides, they're thin, so drawing attention to them is the last thing I want to do. The eyes are the window to the soul, so they should be the focus.

A brush smooths the lengths of my straight chestnut hair. It hangs to the middle of my back where it's cut in the shape of an acorn. My hair is my best feature. It's silky and beautiful and earns me many compliments.

The carpet muffles the sound of my two-inch high, knee-length black leather boots as I make my way down the hall to the elevator. They top off the outfit and add inches to my 5'3" height.

With a low ding, the silver doors ease open, and my breath catches. My blood sinks to my feet as see-thru grey eyes I've only ever admired on my computer screen stare at me live and in person.

Eight months ago, this man standing before me set up a private chat just for us because I had questions about what was expected of me for this event. He's been so helpful. It doesn't hurt that he's a fit man with a solid frame. He dons jeans and a dress shirt in every photo on his social media. In my eyes, he could wear a sweatsuit and look hot enough for a posh event.

A pinch of silver has weaved its way into his thick black hair styled longer on the top with gentle waves but trimmed around his ears. He styles it back as if having effortlessly run his fingers through it after a shower. His skin bears a kiss from the sun on his recent trip to Cancun. It accentuates the grey eyes looking at me from below his eyebrows and burn into the darkest recesses of my soul.

His chin lifts to illuminate striking features as a smile broadens the handsome face. "Well, if it isn't Sky Stone."

Chapter Two

My feet remain stuck to the floor. "*Wolf Black*. W—wow. Um, hi—hi."

He steps forward, grips my wrist, and pulls me into the elevator. Nearly tripping on feet weighted with cinder blocks, I slam against his firm chest.

Strong arms surround me as his warmth seeps through his powder blue dress shirt and onto my cheek. My nipples strain against my bra yearning to sample his heat.

Inhaling deeply, he smells like fresh laundry and leather cologne. My head rests on the thin fabric blocking my cheek from touching his hot skin. His heart beats strong in my ear as I return his hug.

Did he just sniff my hair?

The doors slide shut. We begin to descend before he releases me and steps back against the silver elevator wall while I remain in cement shoes too heavy to lift. My form shivers from the absence of his body heat.

Wolf stands before me looking as illicit as a decadent cake at a Weight Watchers convention. My pussy twitches rudely reminding me that it's been a year since anyone has been in my bed.

Vibrators and dildos are great, but the touch of a strong, warm hand and the deep moans from a man taking his pleasure are infinitely better! Not to mention how the pressure of a solid body is far and above superior to its artificial supplement.

The echo of his deep voice snatches me from my inner monologue. "You're even more beautiful in person."

Why am I trembling? Oh, right; This perfection of a man is going to realize I'm a fraud. I'll be shunned from the writing community for impersonating an author. My writing career will end before it truly begins. He's an *actual* novelist with confidence and success, unlike me. Sure, I write self-publish novels, but am I a *genuine* author?

"Thank you," I whisper as my cheeks flush with embarrassment. "It's great to finally meet you in person."

His fingers fold together at his crotch as his welcoming eyes scan my face. "Yeah. You too. Are you okay? You look a bit flushed."

Fuck! More like Mortified! "Yeah. No, I'm okay. I'm—I'm fine. All's good with me." *For the love of God, shut up!*

Wolf closes in on me and his steamy hand gives my shoulder a little squeeze. He's about to say something, but the doors slide open and his lips close into a slight smile.

Jeez, those eyes could convince a nun to scream, "Fuck me, devil man. Fuck me hard!"

My swallow fails to suppress the little voice inside me insisting that I'm not good enough to be here and to go back to my room, pack up, and go home where I belong.

His hand glides down my spine until a light pressure at the small of my back urges me forward. I don't dare meet his gaze because I'll likely get my heel jammed in the slot on the floor and be pinned in the metal doors.

We step out and the small crowd rushes past us into the waiting elevator. I make it a few feet onto the main floor and my breaths don't come. When did I swallow a bowling ball?

Instead of asking what's wrong, Wolf turns to face me, lifts my chin with his index finger, and stares into my eyes, which doesn't help with my breathlessness. A gentle smile lifts the edges of his lips and light creases edge his eyes. "You're okay. You're going to have fun. These are your peers. They'll welcome you. I promise."

My head shakes as my eyes look away. "I—I just need a minute."

"I've got you. I won't leave you." His finger eases from my chin as his deep voice and penetrating stare hypnotizes me. "Eyes on me, Sky. Breathe."

I follow his instruction by copying his exaggerated intake and exhale of several breaths.

He nods with a smile, steps to my side, and offers me the crook of his arm. My hand slips in and we begin to move. There's no rush to his pace, which pleases me.

As we approach the lounge, laughter and voices grow louder. Some faces I recognize as authors I've chatted with online. My brain seems to have shut off the ability to remember any of their names.

Before we approach, Wolf slows his pace to point to each person in a small gathering near the entrance to whisper their author names to me. Two names are familiar but don't resemble their author photos. Then again, I don't look like mine either.

My author picture has me all made up with make-up thick and perfect and hair curled into a pretty wave. My lip is twisted into a sexy grin and my eyes penetrate through the camera's lens. I love it, but it's not the typical me. They'll never recognize me. Will they be disappointed?

We approach the group, and they all turn to greet us. As they introduce themselves with a handshake or a hug. I smile politely and return their kindness, but more than anything, I'd like to find a dark corner and observe the group rather than interact. What if I say something stupid? I've never been to college or university, like I assume these people have. You can't be a brilliant writer unless you've studied the *'how to'* of it all to extreme. Can you?

Lacy Jace, a NY Times bestselling author of romantic mystery is the first to make me feel included in the group. "Sky Stone… You look just like your photo."

Well, that's a lie.

"Sky, you're more gorgeous in person," Kim J. Kapren adds as her smile widens to reveal imperfect teeth she's hidden from her photos. "How are you? How was your drive up?"

My smile twitches, and I clear my throat. "I'm good. The drive was uneventful." Seems I've found a strong voice.

"That's good. We're so happy to finally meet you!" Lacy says and smothers me in a hug. Her ample bosom and thick arms make for a soft, comforting hug.

"Me too."

She releases me and Wolf's hand presses between my shoulder blades. "Sky's a little nervous. She's never attended an author signing event."

Why would he announce that?

I'm faced with eyebrows lifted and shoulder sags. All at once their voices hum in sympathetic tones as they talk over each other to convince me that I'm going to love this group of people. One swears next year it'll seem like I've come home to family.

She wants me to come again? Do they see me as an equal; a colleague of equal measure? Although I don't know that woman introduced to me by Wolf as Kim C. Baygert, so she likely hasn't followed my struggling author career.

Does everyone go by their author names? Not once has anyone asked for my real name.

***

Over the next two hours, Wolf introduces me to many of the authors. Hopefully, they won't expect me to remember their names tomorrow. Never in my life have I been greeted with so many smiles and hugs by virtual strangers.

Not surprisingly, most of the female authors swoon over Wolf. He's exceptionally handsome and his eyes—as seductive as they are—don't compare to his gentle mannerisms. He didn't outwardly flirt with anyone, but it seemed effortless as he made every woman feel like she was a treasure and each man a stallion in his own right.

As the gentleman he's been all evening, Wolf walks me to my room while we chat about tomorrow's event. After we swap phone numbers, he hugs me longer than what's appropriate for colleagues, but I savour the comfort he offers.

So, I wasn't wrong earlier when I thought he sniffed my hair in the elevator!

All evening my vagina has been slick with need and the battle to shut her up weakens more by the passing seconds I'm in his arms.

His cheek rests on my head and his low voice vibrates my entire body. "By the way, I arranged for our tables to be next to each other. So, if you need any help or a comforting smile, I'll be right there."

A warm sense of relief eases the sinister bees, who haven't stopped fluttering in my tummy for days. I step back and look into his haunting grey eyes and the bees awaken.

"Oh, that's awesome! Wow!" I laugh awkwardly through an exhale as my head bobs and shakes like an idiot. "That's… I—I'm relieved. It's great!"

Shut up and stand still.

The back of my hand brushes from across my forehead to mimic the removal of sweat from a stressful situation and then huff out a breath through puckered lips. *"Whew!"*

It doesn't go unnoticed that his eyes drop to the pucker before his lips pull inward to allow the tip of his tongue to moisten them.

Wolf's head tilts as he takes small steps backward. "Have a good night, Sky. I'll see you downstairs at 8 AM."

After he disappears around the corner, I step inside and close my door, instantly regretting not returning a *good night* sentiment.

This night went a lot better than I had expected. Was it scary, yes, but less so with Wolf next to me.

Tomorrow's another story. Forty-nine other authors will be setting up their tables. Most have experience from years of doing this. At least Wolf will be stationed at the table next to mine.

Mmm, Wolf.

His social media photos had drawn me in but seeing him in person adds an unexpected aura of dominance I hadn't expected. He's gentle when he speaks and in tuned to what I'm feeling, so much so I wonder if he's able to read my mind? No. If he could, he'd have me naked on my bed with his mouth doing inconceivable things to my pussy.

"Oh, for fuck sakes!" I shove away from the door and into the bathroom to prepare for bed.

Chapter Three

My alarm screams far too early. The sun peaks past the gap in the heavy drapes, granting the room a soft hue. I roll to my back and press the base of my palms against my eyelids and rub. They stop and stars dance behind my lids.

While I pee, the dream about Wolf's grey eyes staring down into my eyes while his cock assaulted my vagina urges a wicked smile. Could I ask him to join me in my room tonight after the author's gala? I could, but I shouldn't. He's only being nice to me because he's my friend.

Why would someone as put together as him want someone like me: a woman who freezes in situations most consider fun, a woman who'd rather stay home than see people, a woman who writes her dirties desires but hasn't experienced the heartfelt romantic interludes she boasts on paper? Sex is sex, and I've had plenty, but hubby was my first and he never made me swoon or scream out his name like the women in my books. I'm a fraud, and he's going to realize it.

My hands shake the entire time I get ready. Trying to line my eyes straight was a task I failed at twice before getting it right. Oil massaged into my long locks was all I have the patience for this morning. The initial plan was to curl it, but I don't have the energy for that.

I step into my thong and bounce the girls into the matching black bra. On the way to the closet to put on my low-cut blouse, the bees return.

"I can't do this. Why am I doing this?"

My ass plops on the bed just as my phone startles me with a ring. With my hand glued to my chest, I pick up my phone. The unrecognizable number could be the people managing the event calling to tell me it's cancelled and I can go home.

"Hello."

A voice I've only ever heard yesterday hums through the phone. "Good morning, Sky. How are you doing?"

I swallow to calm the bees, but they vibrate my voice. "Um, I'm—I'm okay. A little nervous."

"How nervous?"

Tears threaten to ruin the make-up I struggled to get right, so I say nothing and squeeze my eyes shut.

"I understand. Will you do something for me?"

My lips remain pinched. "Mhm."

The evenness of his words in the undemanding pitch resumes. "I want you to go to your door and open it enough to swing the safety lock around, and then let the door rest on it, so it won't shut."

My bare feet carry me to the door, and I follow his instruction. "Okay."

"Now, go to your window and open the drapes if they aren't already open."

I stare at the wide windows as they lure me toward them. "They're open."

"A few feet from them, I want you to get down onto your knees facing away from the door. Sit your ass on your heels, and rest the backs of your hands on your thighs."

My gaze drops to my body and my heart pounds until my head spins. He can't see me like this. "But I'm not dressed."

His inhale is loud enough to radiate through the phone's speaker. "What are you wearing?"

It's my turn to suck in a breath to cool my insides. "A bra and panties."

A beat passes before he replies. "That's okay. I'm standing outside your door. Are you on your knees?"

I sink down and place the hand absent the phone on my thigh as he instructed. "I am."

"Tell me to come inside." Strangely, I only hear his voice through the phone and not the gap in the door.

This is it. This is my chance to experience a dominant man. It's obvious he's taken control of this situation. He's given me instructions, and I've followed them without question. Will he fuck me? Will he make me suck his cock?

My words flow with no apprehension. "Come in, Wolf."

"Turn your phone off and set it beside you."

I do, and my hand comes to rest on my thigh, palms up, as he instructed. I can't believe I'm doing this! Is this really happening? If only I could take notes, this would be an impressive scene for one of my books! I could write an entire story around this.

The door eases open and then a loud click fills the room, proof the door has locked. His clothes rustle as he approaches like a tiger to his prey. A hot palm pats my head.

"Good girl." His palm leaves my head, and he steps away.

I try to look over my shoulder to see him—to ask him why he stopped touching me. Does he not like my body?

"Sky, all you have to do right now is breathe." I hear the office chair roll several feet behind me and stop. The faux leather squeaks as he comes to rest on it. "Why are you so nervous?"

"I'm okay. I'm okay." Who am I trying to convince?

"I asked you why, Ms. Stone. Answer my question." When I don't respond, his tone grows more pointed. "Answer my question or I'll punish you."

More than anything, I'd love to test him just to see what he'd do to me, but I won't.

"I don't fit in here. I feel like a fraud. I'm not qualified to be with these people. They have skill and talent I only dream of having. They're New York Times Bestsellers. I'm not! I'm a nobody. I shouldn't be here." My heart pounds loud in my ears and tears threaten to spill.

"Trina, you belong here. If I didn't think you'd fit in, I wouldn't have invited you to attend."

My chin presses to my shoulder, but I don't try to catch a glance of him. "But… How do you know that?"

A slight chuckle begins his reply. "I've read all of your books. You are talented far beyond half of the writers attending today's event."

"But they're bestsellers and I—"

"Have you ever read a book by a world-famous author that was absolutely terrible?" I nod and drop my chin to my chest, and he continues. "Your stories enticed me. The plots are strong, the characters are well-defined, and the sensual scenes are that of fantasies."

"Really? Do you think so?"

I hear Wolf rise and roll the chair back under the desk. He stands so near me his heat warms my naked back.

“I know so.” His palm strokes my head like he would a dog, but I find comfort in it. “Repeat these words: I am good enough to be here. I belong with these people. I am their equal.”

I can’t bring myself to repeat his words. Fingers glide under my hair and it feels great, until his digits curl into a fist with my locks pulling tightly. Using my hair, he urges me to stand, still facing away from him.

Heat from his minty breath brushes over my cheek. “Sky, repeat what I said.”

Wolf’s chest presses to my back and my nipples ache to feel that heat. A solid bulge against my lower back has me fisting my hands to prevent them from reaching to discover it.

My voice quivers; not from anxiety but arousal, and a full breath comes between sentences. “I’m good enough to be here. I belong with these people and I’m their equal.”

My brows furrow and my body stiffens when his free hand palms my pudgy tummy.

He tugs my hair to tip my head away from his. A kiss unlike any I could describe in words presses to my nape. My skin prickles like a wave overcoming me and my knees weaken.

Holding me tight against what I believe to be his dress shirt and jeans, he whispers, “Put your fingers in your panties and massage your clit.”

Ooooh! Here we go!

My pause meets another kiss on my neck, nearer to my ear. "Would you rather my fingers touch you?"

With a mind of its own, my head nods.

"If you want me to stop for any reason, say red. Do you understand?

Again, I nod. My breaths come so fast my throat has dried and I can't swallow.

My body stills completely when his index finger slips between my labia, over my clitoris, and dips into the wetness he's earned.

"Mm, Ms. Stone is soaked for Mr. Black."

Oh, my God! Yes!

Slick with my arousal, his middle finger returns to my swollen clitoris. His index and ring finger pinch outside my labia and hold my pussy like a taco around his middle finger. They tug slightly and it's uncomfortable but adds to the sensation gained from the tiny circles he brushes over my clit. Tingles rush through me and I'm lighter than air.

Using my hair, Wolf tugs my head back against his shoulder before setting the strands free. His hand wraps around my throat. Slight pressure holds me firmly against him.

Panic urges my hands to grip his forearm.

Fight or flight? Fight or flight?

The pressure against my clitoris grows firmer.

No fight. No flight.

Warm, needy words in a sensual tone vibrate me from the outside in. "You are so beautiful. The flow of your stories arouses me. I can't tell you how many times I fantasized you were the female and me the male in those precarious situations." A soft moan vibrates my neck. "To see your face lit with passion just before an orgasm overwhelms you—an orgasm *I* granted you—had me gripping myself for relief. Believe me when I tell you that you are an incredible writer. Nobody's words get me off like yours do."

My body quivers as the fullness in my lower tummy grows tighter. He has my pussy tiptoeing toward the edge of bliss. This man knows the inner workings of a woman.

I'm so fucking close!

His finger pauses and lifts away and my hips buck forward to give chase.

"Tsk tsk. Not yet, pretty girl." Kisses to my neck divert my attention away from my furious pussy. "Tell me you're beautiful."

"You're beautiful."

I feel his smile before hearing it in his breath. "Come on. *You* are beautiful, not me."

"No. You *are* beautiful. You're so—" My words fail when Wolf's hand juts further into my panties until his finger dips into my vagina. Before I can moan, another joins it and his palm presses against my stiff clitoris.

My moan sounds more whimpered than pleasured. “Please. Oh, Wolf, please.”

He fucks me with fingers arched toward the front, hitting something inside me that shoots pleasure directly to my clitoris as his palm brushes over the nub each time his fingers penetrate me.

“Do you want to cum, little girl?” His teeth nip my ear.

“Yes. Fuck, yes!” Moans ride each panted breath.

My eyelids part, but the room is so bright it threatens to steal me from the fantasy that can’t be really happening. They pinch closed and the floating sensation resumes.

A third finger dips into me as his hand pulls tighter to my throat.

“Tell me you’re worthy of a successful career and then you can take your pleasure.”

It’s difficult to move, to breathe, to find the ability to speak, but I need to. “I’m—I’m worthy of a—a successful ca—career.”

“Cum for me,” he whispers so seductively it sends me plummeting into darkness.

I’m swallowed up while shattering into a million pieces. There’s nothing but my clitoris and his fingers. Spinning and floating in a pain so delicious it’s unmatched. I want to remain in this state for all of eternity, but too soon I’m yanked back to reality. My body jerks each time the tip of his drenched finger brushes over my satiated, swollen clitoris.

Every muscle in my body aches in a sensational exhaustion as serotonin floats through my veins. We remain motionless with his hand spanned over my lower tummy as my breathing slows. His other arm holds firmly across my upper chest to prevent my noodle legs from dropping my carcass to the floor.

A few moments pass before Wolf's hand seeks my shoulder and urges me to face him. His cheeks are flushed and his parted lips swollen and slightly darker pink than I know them to be.

He stares at me through glassy eyes with wide pupils. "How do you feel?"

With my bottom lip tucked in my teeth, I blink several times before my words come. "I—that was, um—wow! Yeah, ah… I'm good."

The fingers that recently surrounded my neck cradle the back of my head. "But are you relaxed?"

My eyes widen as my mouth gapes to fill my lungs. "Yeah. Very. Thank you."

Realizing he needs relief, too, I reach for his belt, but his hand covers mine.

"No. This was about you." He places a lingering kiss to my forehead as he breathes in the scent of my hair. "I'll see you downstairs in half an hour."

Should I be disappointed that he resisted my favour? Because I'm not. Sure, I want to put an image to the bulge that pressed against my back. Is he shy because he has a small penis? I wouldn't care either way; the man is a wet dream walking.

Wolf strides out the door, and the click of the automatic lock snaps me back to reality. Did that really happen?

The mirror to my side proves the pinkness of my neck from where he held me. It won't linger for very long, so I appreciate the beauty of it while it lasts.

Half an hour.

"Shit!"

I rush to touch up my make-up with unsteady hands while smiling like a fool. Instead of being nervous, I'm excited to go to the event hall just to see him again. Will he act like nothing happened and shoot me a wink when nobody's looking, or will he swoop me into his arms no matter who sees?

He never kissed me. He masturbated me but didn't kiss me. Maybe the two hours between the event and the author's gala will be spent rolling around in the sheets with Wolf. Then again, this may have been a one-time thing, and we'll return to just being friends, never mentioning what just happened. Strangely, I'm okay with either scenario.

Wolf made me understand that I belong. I've never claimed my worth, let alone say it out loud for someone else to hear. Even though they were his words, hearing myself say them changes everything. I still have doubts, but the panic isn't there.

With a renewed sense of confidence having taken its place, I'll forever be grateful to him.

Chapter Four

With an added hop in my step, I roll my wagon filled with books, swag, and everything I'll need to set up a sexy showcase to draw in potential readers.

A man with a lanyard around his neck with a nametag swinging asks my name and hands me one with my name in bold lettering with the word 'author' written beneath. I slip it over my neck as the woman beside him lifts her clipboard and tells me I'm at table 42.

Authors with wagons are shuffling about, either laughing or wearing wide eyes to prove their newbies, like me. Only, my eyes show little fear as they skirt from one table to the next, seeking Mr. Wolf Black.

The second aisle of tables near the far end is table 45. It's just a table, but soon it'll reveal a lot of the books I've put so much effort into.

An author I don't know is at the table to my left, but we're courteous and friendly in our greeting. She's occupied with her set-up, as are so many men and women with swinging lanyards.

I'm quick to set up my table; arranging and rearranging until it suits me. The table next to me is still vacant. Did Wolf decide not to come? Is he trying to avoid me? Worry threatens to steal my confidence.

With my purse in hand, I smile at each person beaming back at me and make my way to the washroom. The lights are bright on my face as I stare at my perfectly made-up eyes.

The door swings open, and two women enter. They're laughing as one's hips sway wildly, imitating something humorous. They pause and smile before they walk past me toward the stalls.

One's husky voice says, "Good morning. You're Sky Stone, right? This is your first event?"

She recognizes me? I nod and try to read her name on her lanyard, but it's flipped backward.

She asks, "Are you all set up?"

My hands run beneath the water even though I didn't use a stall. "I think so. Yes."

The other author asks, "Are you nervous? I hope not. You're going to do great. Your covers are smoking hot, so that'll draw buyers to your table."

"Hopefully." I pull a scratchy paper sheet from the roll to dry my hands.

"You'll do great," the other says as she spins toward the stalls and disappears behind a door.

One more glance at my reflection and a tug at the hem of my shirt has my chin up and a deep breath holding in my lungs. *I've got this!*

I slide unnoticed past a small group of giddy authors by keeping my face tilted toward my phone in hand. All I want to do is sit behind my table for a few moments of peace before they open the doors to the public and an impossibly stressful few hours ensue.

As I sit, a movement catches my eye. Mr. Wolf. He holds three of his books in hand as he watches me. My face flushes and I can't help but smile like a fucking idiot with my face scrunched awkwardly. I must be fifty shades of red!

"How are you, Ms. Stone? Your set up looks great." His voice, although fading into the surrounding chaos, is deep as it laps at my ears.

The way he stands with his shoulders squared and head tipped forward just enough where his eyes burn me from beneath his brows sends a tingle to my nether region. What he did to me has burned into my memory forever. I can still feel him touch me while his breath caresses my neck.

I say nothing, fearing my voice won't work anyway, so my lips pucker as I nod.

He leans forward and whispers, "Cat got your tongue?"

Before I can speak, a man in his mid-fifties with grey hair and a long beard walks past my table and puts his hand out to greet Wolf. "Hey, you. I haven't seen you in a while. How the hell are you?"

With wide smiles, the men hug with a slap to their back as men do.

I don't recognize the man, so I look down at my phone to shoot a text to my mom letting her know I'm all set up and ready to go. She'll give me a pep talk by telling me I'm an amazing author, and then she'll insist I have a great time and call her later.

As expected, a rapid-fire text comes back, but before I can read it, Wolf calls to me. "Sky Stone, I'd like you to meet Andrew C. Gatts."

I stand and stretch my arm toward him as he steps forward with a wide smile to accept. "It's nice to meet you. Wolf has told me so much about you."

My back straightens and my hands clasp together at my belly button. "*Really?* You have?"

Wolf nods and says, "Only the good things."

"Since you were given high praise, I've read a few of your books. You're incredibly talented. I'm surprised nobody's picked you up yet."

"Picked me up?" Confusion pinches my brows as my head wavers to the right. My brain suddenly wakes up and my mouth widens into a silent O.

"A publishing company," he says and clears his throat. "Would you consider writing a book together?"

Seriously?! This man I don't know, who carries himself with high dignity, wants to write a book with me? Am I a talented author? Am I really?

"Oh, um. I've never cowritten before, but I'd consider it." My thoughts scramble about how that would even happen. Will he laugh at me when he realizes I'm small potatoes in the book world? So many questions: Would he write a chapter, and I write the next? Would one of us write while the other gives ideas? How humiliated will I be when I ask him a hundred questions?

His voice is soft as he nods and raises his hand as if able to read my jumbled thoughts. "I'll contact you in a month or so. Think about it. First, read some of my work to see if you think we'd be a good fit. I think we have the potential to kick out a trophy book that will linger in the charts."

All I can do is glance from one man to the next until he turns back to Wolf, reaches for his hand to exchange greetings before he walks a few tables down to talk to another author.

"Who? Um, who is that?" I take two steps toward Wolf and he does the same. We stand a step away and his scent doesn't escape my deep inhale.

"I'll send you his links, so you can look him up. If I were you, I'd jump on his offer. He's an award-winning romance erotica author."

“How come I’ve never heard of him?” I ask without expecting an answer.

“Maybe you’re too busy writing to look up now and then.” My face tilts up to see him smirking. “But how are you doing? Are you nervous?”

My face flushes as I look down at my fingers fidgeting at my waist. “I wasn’t, but now that we’re standing this close, I’m a bit nervous.”

“Nervous or aroused?” he asks in a low whisper to keep the author behind us from overhearing.

A deep breath raises my breasts, which directs his attention to my cleavage. “Both, I suppose. I should thank you for earlier.”

“No need to thank me. I enjoyed that as much as you did, and I’m glad I could be there to help.”

My thumbnail nips between my teeth, but Wolf gently grips my wrist and lowers my arm while scolding me with his eyes.

He releases my hand and says, “Sit with me at the dinner tonight.”

“Yeah, of course.” I tuck hair behind my ear and return behind my table and avoid his eyes so he doesn’t see my disappointment. I was hoping we’d spend the two hours between the event and the celebration dinner in my room, naked, and fucking like there’s no tomorrow. Basically, for *us*, there is no tomorrow. He has a life hours away from mine. Neither of us could walk away from our careers and start anew. It's just not feasible. So, we have today. That's all, and I was hoping to make the most of it.

A female voice higher than what's pleasant rings over the loudspeaker. "Hello, authors! Is everyone set up and ready to go?" A lot of hoots and whistles light up the room and the excitement is infectious. "If we can get all the authors into the main corridor, we'd love to get a picture of everyone together. It'll be posted online in a matter of minutes for everyone to pick up and boast on their social media to bring more people in. In ten minutes, we'll open the doors to the public. Are you excited?"

More wild calls sing out and the authors make their way to the corridor. Wolf reaches for my hand and I slip mine into his without thinking.

He guides me with the crowd until we're squished into a large huddle.

The photographer calls out, "Smile. Three, two—" and Wolf's hand grips my ass cheek and squeezes, startling me. "Okay, let's take another."

I glare up at Wolf. His quirked brow and childish grin make me laugh loudly. Two oblivious authors turn to look at me while smiling, and Wolf chuckles. His hand is still on my ass, and I hope nobody behind us is paying attention.

“Three, two, one… Thanks everyone. Have a great event!”

The crowd grows loud as it disperses and we all funnel back into the room and to our tables.

***

The event goes well even though I don’t sell more than a dozen books. I hadn’t expected I would, but the experience made the expense worthwhile. Chatting with readers and watching their excitement about meeting authors uplifted my spirit like nothing has before. Some people hold authors in high regard for the hard work they do, and they made me feel special. Nobody’s ever made me feel special, not like this—and moms don’t count.

Chapter Five

Hours later, the crowds have dwindled to only a few stragglers rushing from table to table hoping to purchase as many books as they can before they're kicked out. I flop in my chair and let out the biggest sigh I can manage.

A shrill squeal shreds my eardrums just before a woman's voice roars through the loudspeaker. "Oh, shoot. Sorry, folks. That was loud. Authors, that's all she wrote, so to speak. The doors will be closing in five minutes, and you can begin to pack up. We hope to see all of you at the dinner at five o'clock. Thanks for making this event so great, and we hope you had a wonderful time. See you all later."

Clapping, hoots, and whistles ignite and my arms rise over my head to join in the celebration.

I'm quiet as I pack up my table and arrange everything in my wagon so it won't fall out. One more glance around to make sure I forgot nothing, and then turn to see Wolf's ass as he bends to pick up a box of books from beneath his table. He stands as he turns toward me and sets the box in his wagon.

“Hey. Are you looking at my ass?” His tone is serious and his lowered brows might agree, but the crooked grin gives him away.

“Yes. Actually, I was.” A chuckle raises my shoulders.

“Interesting.” He slowly approaches and drops his eyes to my chest. “I’m going to put my things in my room, take a quick shower, and dress in what I’ll be wearing to the dinner. After that, I’m free until five o’clock. I wonder what I can do to fill the time in between?”

Palms up, my arms rise at my sides as my wide eyes prove innocence by skirting about the room. “What ever can we do to fill that time? Hmm.” My finger presses to my chin. “I plan to return to my room, take a shower, and lie in my bed nude for about an hour before I need to get dressed and ready for the dinner.”

His tongue coats his lips, and he clears his throat. “I’ll be standing at your door in thirty minutes. Let me in or don’t. It’s your choice. Either way, I still hope you’ll sit with me during dinner.”

The coffee in my tummy does a somersault and threatens to make a hasty reappearance, but I swallow it down. As I turn away from him, I flip my hair over my shoulder and tease in my best southern belle accent, “Whatever will we do if I open the door?”

***

Fifteen minutes later, I'm back in my room and stripping. I shower shockingly quick despite needing the scrape of a razor to regain my feminine softness. Wearing only a towel with my toothbrush jutting from my pursed lips, there's a tap at my door.

He's here.

I spit, rinse, and swallow a gulp of cold water to settle the tension in my tummy. My fingers glide beneath my eyes to erase the slight slide of make-up from the shower's heat.

Deep breath.

My hand grips the door handle and I startle when there's another gentle rap on the door.

Wolf's deep, growly whisper rumbles through the thick wooden door. "I'm going to huff, and puff, and blow this door down, Ms. Stone."

Leave it to him to ease my tension with a suitable nursery rhyme. I ease the door open and lean my weight on my left leg and rest my free hand on my waist over the fluffy white towel. "This little piggy wouldn't want that, Wolf."

Grey eyes bore into me from below his brows. His flushed lips are parted as if hungry to ravish me.

His head slowly tips up to drink me in, as if imagining me less the towel. "Well, now, Ms. Stone. You look good enough to eat."

My eyes lift to the right. “You’re mixing up your nursery rhymes, Mr. Black.”

He steps forward, but stops at the doorframe. “Invite me in.”

“And now you’re a vampire?” My arm flops at my side.

The top two buttons on his black dress shirt remain unfastened, and his black jeans are trimmed with a thick leather belt. But his boots grab my attention. They’re polished black, with a sharp silver toe—masculine as much as footwear can be.

His lips twitch to suppress a smile. “Bloodsucking isn’t my thing, but I can’t promise not to bite.”

I’m strangely calm as grey eyes drink me in with a mix of salacious need and jovial comedy. “In that case, do come in, vampire Wolf.”

All I can do is gasp when he rushes me, wraps his arms around me, and plants his lips on mine with a ravenous fury. The door closes with a loud click as he rushes me backward until I’m lying on my back on the bed with him between my legs. His kiss doesn’t ease and I know my lips will be puffy and sore later, but *Oh. My. God.* This is smut novel worthy!

He suddenly straddles my hips on his knees, feeds his hand into my hair and pulls me into a sitting position. His crotch is at my neck, and I watch as his fingers work the buckle to his belt, open the button on his pants, and lower the zipper.

"Watching you at the event, all I could think of was how much I want to watch those beautiful lips wrap around my cock. So, I'm going to fuck that pretty mouth, and then I'm going to spank you until your ass is red hot. Do you understand?"

My nod reminds me of his grip on my hair.

Telling me he's going to fuck my mouth is the dirties, sexiest thing any man has ever said to me. But when he said he'd spank me, I swear cat-calls erupted from my vagina to urge him on, but that may have just been in my imagination.

I can't look away as the anticipation of what he'll pull from his jeans has my heart pounding everywhere except my chest.

Wolf's fist hugs his thick, rigid cock as a dot of pre-cum on the bulbous head catches the light.

My teeth pinch my lower lip as he pulls my hair to tip my head.

"Open your mouth and let me see how deep it is to your throat." He moans when I open wide for his inspection. "Now be a good girl and take my cock as deep as you can."

He aims my mouth over the tip of his cock and eases his grip enough where I'll have control over how deep I take him, and I can't look away from his face. His chest expands when the head of his cock brushes past my lips and over my wet tongue.

A forced exhale carries a deep moan as he watches his entire shaft sink into my mouth and down my throat.

I've been told I'm very good at swallowing cock. My ex taught me how to do it without choking. At least he was good for something.

With his unbelievably tight ass held firmly in my grip, I push his hips forward as my head bobs over his shaft. Tears drip from the edges of my eyes with my efforts to take all of him.

My hair is yanked back and his mouth smashes over mine. His tongue dances with mine for only a moment before he abruptly slides off my legs and stands on the floor. Using my hair, he directs me to stand before spinning me to face away, releasing my hair, and forcing me chest down on the mattress. The toe of his boots urge my feet wide apart.

Either excitement or anxiety has my blood racing through my veins at a deafening pitch. My hands fist the comforter as I await what he'll do next. Will he suddenly spank me or ease into it? How does one ease into a spanking?

A hot palm rests on my right ass cheek. The mattress at my waist sags beneath the weight from his knee, and his other palm spans my upper back. The heat spreads across both cheeks as he tenderly strokes them.

Swat!

"*Oh! Wha— Fuck!*" My breaths rush in quick gasps. I swallow and try to look over my shoulder as a smile teases my lips. "More?"

Another spank and my pussy burns with need. Surely I'm sick in the head or something is wrong with me to enjoy being spanked. The pain sucks, but I've never been so aroused. Each spank sends me to another level of need until the bed sways beneath me and I need to grip it with all of my strength to keep from flying off.

A scream in my voice shocks me. "Fuck me! Please, fuck me!"

The bed shifts and his hand weaves into my hair as he takes his position behind me. In one rushed thrust, he's buried deep inside me. The strain on my walls is intense, but exactly what I needed.

His whisper growls above me. "Oh, fuck, Sky. You feel so fucking good."

Wolf thrusts like a demon with a day-pass. Each time he impales me, his violent grunts grow louder.

My thoughts blur as each breath screams from my soul as he forcefully thrusts into my body. It feels so goddamn good! It's been too long since I've been so full it's hard to breathe.

Three erratic thrusts laced with barbaric whimpers precede him pulling free from my pussy only to force his cock slick with my juices between my ass cheeks. He humps as if he were inside me before his body stiffens and he falls silent.

Seconds pass as only my gasping breaths sing about the room. He collapses forward as his lungs empty. He swallows loudly before his hot gasps warm my spine.

Wolf grips my hips and spins me until I'm flat on my back with my feet on the floor. His face is flushed and his eyes are slits as he sinks onto his knees. His hands grip under my knees and raise my thighs up to my abdomen.

When his hands ease down my inner thighs toward my pussy, I grip under my knees to hold my thighs against my chest, leaving me fully exposed and vulnerable.

Wolf laps from my pucker through the folds of my dripping wet vagina, and sucks my clit as his tongue ravishes the needy button.

Oh, yes!

Fingers from each hand work into my vagina and pull my cavity open. The stretch is immense and slightly painful, but so fucking delicious. My head sways side to side as my hips rock to match the lapping of his tongue and suction from his mouth over my clit. His fingers pull and release, pull and release as if hoping I'll open wider and wider each time. Perhaps I am because I feel wide enough to take on a commercial truck.

The world spins and I fist the comforter with all of my strength to keep from lifting off the mattress and floating to the heavens. Blackness envelops me and everything stops, everything except the violent pounding of my heart. I don't feel myself gyrating beneath his mouth, but I am. My lungs burn for oxygen, but I can't manage it—I don't want to. A breath will awaken me from this glory, and what a pity that will be. But a breath finds me and awakens me to reality.

A hazy Wolf kisses my lips as my vision clears enough where I can kiss him back. He sits me up and sinks back onto his knees on the floor.

"Thank you, Sky," he whispers as his palm coasts down my flushed cheek. "You're so beautiful, strong, and delicious."

Words are foreign to me as my brain swims with serotonin, so I nod like a fucking idiot.

He smiles, kisses my forehead, and stands to fasten his pants as he makes his way to the bathroom. The tap runs and shuts off before he comes back into view.

"How do you feel?" he asks and leans his shoulder on the wall with his hands on his hips. "Are you calm?"

I nod and swallow before a childish smile invades my maturity. "Yes. Very calm. That was—"

“Fantastic?” he adds and smiles just as childlike. “If you agree, I should go unless you need me.”

“Need you?” For? I can brush my own hair, shower unaided, and even put my clothes on without assistance.

“If you need me or want me to escort you downstairs, I’ll stay.” After I shake my head, he tilts his head before standing tall. “You have my phone number. If you need anything, call, and I’ll come.”

I look at the clock on the nightstand and appreciate his concern for me. “I’m thoroughly relaxed now, so I think I’ll be okay. I’ll see you downstairs in half an hour.”

“Friends forever?” he asks.

“Nothing more, nothing less.” My smile is soft and genuine as my palms press onto the mattress on either side of my hips.

“Nothing more, nothing less.” With a wink and a smirk, Wolf turns and leaves.

The room is silent as I sit nude at the edge of the bed and try to burn what just happened into my memory forever.

Wolf gave me the gift of strength and positivity to get through my first book signing event, and for that, I will forever be grateful. We’ll have dinner with the other authors and continue our friendship, but our union stops there. Who knows what the future holds? Maybe the universe will decide otherwise, maybe not. Either way, I'll cherish this weekend for the rest of my life.

~ *The End* ~

Don't leave just yet! A teaser for THE WIDOWED, book Two in the Rule Breakers standalone series, is on the next page.
But first:
Please take a moment to rate this book and/or leave a review.
Your review helps readers distinguish the good books from the bad.

The Widowed

INTERNATIONAL BESTSELLING AUTHOR

PEBBLES LACASSE

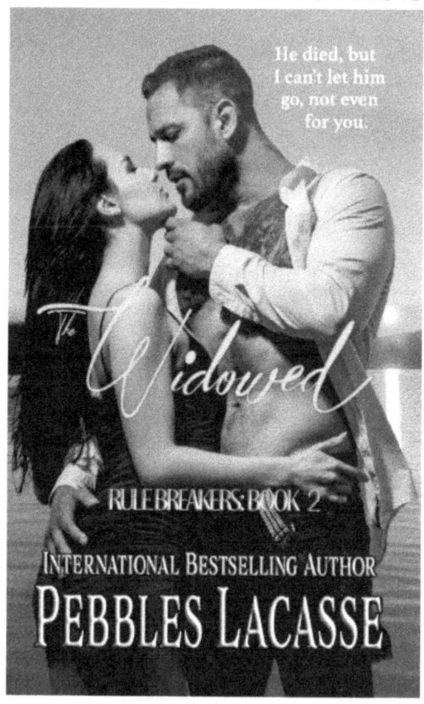

CHAPTER ONE

Heather

A wisp of wind tickles my cheek.

Leo and I are standing at the altar. We gaze into each other's swimming eyes just before he leans in toward me. Thick fingers brush a cascading tear from my flushed cheek before circling behind my neck. His smile fades just before his lips press to mine, but the heat from the passion in his kiss doesn't leave me questioning how much he loves me.

This is when I wake, every time.

We never get to walk back down the aisle. I never throw the bouquet or dance with my father. But the proof lives in my memories, videos, and photos. They're readily available to peruse whenever my heart needs a reminder of that perfect day.

"Good morning, Mouse." Leo presses a kiss to my head before his arm lifts from my waist and he rolls to his back. A rushed inhale precedes his yowling yawn. It's undeniable that he's stretching his limbs by the way the bed shakes from the protest of stiff muscles.

He's been chopping and stacking firewood for next year's winter. Logs burn better after drying for a year before use. Since this is the only way we heat our home, it's an unavoidable chore. Thankfully, Leo is a solid man with a strong back, despite being well into his forties.

"Do you have more wood to split?" I sit up and raise my hands over my head for my stretch. I haven't been chopping wood, but I've been helping to stack it, and that's hard on my back.

Leo's twice my weight and at least twenty times stronger. While he carries half a dozen logs at a time, I can carry two—at the most. After half an hour of doing that, I'm gasping for breath and eager to sit and watch him continue. He doesn't complain when I quit; he laughs and calls me a wimpy mouse.

"Mouse" is Leo's nickname for me. When we were dating, he knighted me with it using a strand of red licorice at the local movie theatre. I'm barely 5'1" tall and weigh 120 pounds after a hefty meal. He's 6'1" tall and averages 220 pounds before a good meal. People have said we look hilarious together. They assume he always has the final say in everything we do, but they couldn't be more wrong. When it comes down to it, I'm the one with the TNT attitude, especially when I know

I'm right. Leo's laid back, which is a godsend. If he were more aggressive in his nature, we'd bump heads all the time and wouldn't fit so perfectly together.

A muffled grumble slips from Leo as he stands and stretches onto his toes. He shakes out his arms while his head tips from shoulder to shoulder and he says, "Yeah, but there isn't much left to do. It shouldn't take more than an hour."

I slip my arms into the sleeves of my soft blue bathrobe as I round the bed. My arms encircle his waist. "Do you want me to help?"

His wide hands stroke my robe-covered upper back and arms. "Nope. I'll move quicker if I don't have to worry about tripping over you or tossing a chunk of wood your way. That wouldn't be good. You don't need any damage to that little brain of yours."

He snickers when I lightly punch his sides. "Little brain? As opposed to… what, your massive brain?"

"Yup!" His stomach tightens with silent laughter.

"Just because your body's bigger doesn't mean your thicker brain can retain more information than mine. I mean, mine might have more highways to retrieve said information, whereas yours is likely a block of grey matter too dense to retrieve information."

"I think that was an insult, but my block of grey matter can't decipher," he taps my temple with his finger, *"woman-thinking."*

My head tips back to gaze up at him as he looks down at me. "You don't want to think like a woman. There is nothing but chaos going on in here."

"I prefer my man-brain. We have one thought at a time which—in my opinion—makes us more efficient."

"Efficient? At only one task at a time, sure. Women can do ten things at once while thinking about the next twenty tasks we need to complete."

Leo's brows lift as he sucks air through his teeth. "I'll gladly place the crown on your head if I don't have to think like that. It sounds painful."

My face contorts. "Sometimes, yeah. It is."

He whimpers as his bottom lip protrudes to show some pity. "So, what are your plans for today?"

Leo tenderly brushes a stray hair from my forehead, reminding me how much this man loves me, and I love him. What did I do well enough to earn such a reward?

"I have some running around to do. What do you want for dinner?"

He shrugs without releasing me from his hold. "I don't care."

My shoulders round as my arms drop to my sides and I voice my complaint in a pouty tone. “I’m wounded. You were supposed to say *me*. You want *me* for dinner.”

His warm hand feeds through my hair and he leans down until his lips are an inch from mine. “Mouse, you are not a simple main course. You are the savoury dessert worth waiting for.”

With brows raised, my voice worthy of innocence grows without effort. “Flattery will get you everywhere with me, Mr. Davis.”

He pecks a kiss to my puckered lips before sauntering to the bathroom with a swagger in his step and shuts the door.

While I wait for my turn in the washroom, I strip the bedding and stuff the sheets in the hamper. Since the sheets got a little sweaty and carry too much of our DNA, swapping them for a fresh set is wise. Is there anything better than sliding our bodies bearing a day’s worth of exhaustion between the cool sheets of a freshly made bed? I think not.

Last night, Leo rocked my world; as he does almost every night. After he licked my pussy until I had to slap his forehead to get him to stop torturing my hypersensitive clit, he flopped on his back so I could ride him. It’s my second favourite position. His back was sore from chopping wood, so doing the work myself benefited both of us.

My head shakes even though nobody is here to see me. *Work?* Riding Leo is not work, not in the conventional sense.

My absolute favourite position is with us both standing with my hands against the wall while he fucks me from behind until he lifts me off my feet with his powerful thrusts. He usually ends up gripped onto my hips and lifting until my feet are off the floor. That way he can straighten his thighs to get some relief from being spread with bent knees. It's not my fault Leo's a giant.

I toss the sheets and a few dirty towels in the washer but wait until after I've had my shower to run the cycle.

***

"Okay, I'm off," I say as my runners pad the path down toward the garage where Leo is outside finishing up with the log-splitter.

He turns and smiles as he sets a fat log on the splitter. "I'll see you when you get home. Drive safely."

We share a quick kiss. As I turn to walk away, he grabs my arm and pulls me back for another kiss, this one more passionate than the last. Even after being together for seven years and married for five, the passion between us remains intense.

It's just Leo and me. We agreed to hold off on having children for a few years. One day we'll have little Leos and Heathers, just not now.

Having nobody other than our hound, Georgie, to tend to, nothing has kept us from taking our bi-yearly vacations. We live north of Thessalon, Ontario in Canada. We love it here but it's slow-moving, and sometimes we need to shake it up a bit. Twice a year we choose a destination by taping a map to the living room wall and flipping a coin to see who gets to put the mask on, spin once, and throw the dart to choose our next vacation destination. We've been to Australia, Western Canada, Mexico, two states in America, Italy, and Jamaica. Maybe this year Scotland will attract the head of the dart. I hope so!

The drive south on Highway 129 calms me. There aren't many cars travelling these miles of road, especially in the fall. Summer is busier with tourists and bikers. Quite a few motorcycles travel this highway because of the Tail of the Dragon tour. Motorcyclists of all breeds experience the freedom and beauty of northern Ontario. Highway 129 begins in Thessalon and heads due north to Chapleau. There isn't much in the means of excitement happening around here, but the ride north is a beautiful one a person will never forget.

The bikers are always polite, obey the rules of the road, and are respectful of the locals. Some take the time to tell the tales of their life's struggles and what led them to our tiny town. Some say the Tail of the Dragon is known worldwide and that bikers dream of riding their bikes through these mountains.

Many local folks say the noise pollutes the serenity of the great north. But I love to hear the rumble of the bikes as they sail over the stretch of highway. Their boisterous roars travel over the trees all the way to our property. I can just imagine how stimulating it must be to have that powerful vibration quiver between my legs as the wind whips past my cheeks. Thrilling! But it'll never happen.

For one thing, I don't know how to ride a two-wheeled bike. The thought of learning how to drive makes me queasy. I have shitty balance on two legs—two wheels would be terrifying. Plus, Leo believes bikes are too dangerous and won't risk losing me.

Four-wheeled ATVs are the extent of my wild adventures. Put me on one of those, and I'll show off my freaky driving skills. I can climb steep mountain trails, and do often. Especially when Leo and I challenge each other.

We have many trails on our 1,084-acre property. Our favourite is the one leading to the rear of the small lake where Leo loves to go fishing with Georgie by his side. The second path to the right offers a rocky climb on the ATVs, and it's a riot. Leo flipped his two-years ago. He jumped free and all was good, except for the brake line and some scratches on the rear quarter panel. It could have been so much worse.

Despite the dangerous adventures we get into, we love the thrill too much to stop.

We also own the property surrounding the small lake. Since trespassing is illegal, the lake is secluded so we call it ours even though nobody can technically own a body of water.

Making love on the boulders after a swim is a common occurrence for us. Afterward, we sun ourselves while we enjoy a picnic we bring with us. Being there allows us a few hours where we can be free of our daily stresses to enjoy each other's company.

The small grocery store in town isn't too busy today. Sometimes it's difficult to get around with a cart because the aisles are narrow enough where two can barely pass side by side without knocking something off a shelf. The store has almost all the basics we may need between our monthly trips into the big city. The city trips consist of a long drive with multiple stores visited, but we always treat ourselves to something fun while we're there. We often see a movie, have a nice dinner, see a play, or just enjoy the simple pleasure of an ice cream on a hot day.

Today, I need only the basics: milk for our coffee and tea, butter for the cookies I plan to bake, and all the ingredients needed to make a huge pot of chili. Every fall I make a massive amount of chili, scoop it into plastic-ware, and set them in the deep freezer. After a long day of plowing snow with the tractor, shovelling what can't be plowed, and caring for everything else that needs tending to when you live in the outskirts of civilization, a ready-made meal zapped to steaming in the microwave is exactly what our chilled-to-the-bone bodies require.

A soft voice behind me steals my attention from calculating how many cans of kidney beans I'll need for the batch.

"Hello, Heather. How've you been?"

Belinda Jerice glides her palm over her salt and pepper hair pulled into a taught bun to ensure not a strand has dared to escape.

Not allowing me to respond—not that I expected she would—she leans over the handle of her cart. I lean in so I'll hear what gossip she's about to whisper.

"Did you hear what happened to Alicia?" Her brows rise as her jaw pulls to her neck. She doesn't give me a chance to tell her how uninterested I am in gossip. "Alicia was caught kissing *Amy*. Can you believe it? Greg and Mia saw them in Amy's car. Apparently, it was *very* heated." Her head moves on a swivel as she glances over her shoulder. "They said there may have been some heavy petting going on, but they couldn't see to be certain."

"Uh-huh," I mumble and change the subject. "So, how's your son doing?"

Her son, Jim, is a bit of a sore topic for Belinda. He moved to Vancouver last year. He was the last of her four children to leave the nest. They had a big blowout at the yearly fireworks show last summer, and everyone heard his rant. At thirty-two-years-old, he'd had enough of her trying to run his life. She wouldn't stop nagging him about everything she deemed him doing wrong. He snapped and let his frustrations flow out like a waterfall, embarrassing her while people stared.

"He's fine!" she snaps before her feeble attempt at a smile quickly sags. "Well, I should let you get back to it. Making chili, are you?"

My mouth opens to confirm such as the two cans of kidney beans I'm holding draw my eyes.

"Chili is so good. You know, you can freeze chili in baggies. It's a great way to—"

My voice fades into the background when the bell over the door dings, capturing my attention. Two men walk in with smiles on their faces. One I recognize as Kirk Greer, but the other man younger and damn good looking—I haven't seen before. Who is he, and why is he with Mr. Greer?

Belinda is vicious when she pokes my shoulder with her sharp fingernail. "Heather!"

Ouch! That'll leave a bruise.

"I was talking to you. What has you so…" Her voice trails off as she turns to see where I'm looking. "Oh, that's Kirk's son, Dane."

"I didn't know Mr. Greer had a son." And a sexy one at that! Stop drooling; you're married to an amazing man you're deeply in love with.

"He's here visiting his father. That might be because Kirk looks like he hasn't been well, but nobody seems to know anything. I've asked him if he's sick, but he insists he's fine and tells me to stay out of other people's business. He can be so rude." Her hands grip the bar on her shopping cart and her head shakes as if she's horribly insulted anyone would talk to her that way. "He's never been so rude to me. I don't know what I did to make him so sensitive."

You won't shut up about everyone's business but your own.

"I'm sure if he wanted *everyone* to know, he'd tell you," I say and mean the innuendo, but she lets it fly over her head, not picking up on my insult.

"I suppose so. I'll get it out of him. Maybe I'll ask Dane. He might need a little consoling if his father's ill. Maybe he'll want to talk about it to get it off his chest."

His chest? It looks strong beneath that crimson hoodie.

Oh, my God! Heather! Stop it!

"I should get back to it," I say and set six big cans in my cart. Do I need six cans? Probably not.

"Yes, of course." Belinda leans in again and lowers her voice. "If you find out anything, be sure to let me know."

I suck air between my teeth as I step back, not saying I will or I won't. Kirk Greer himself could tell me all the details of his illness, and I'd never tell her anything. Whatever she hears—truth or not—spreads quicker than a wildfire.

My focus is on my shopping list and not the eye-candy strolling around the store with his father. I may be married to the best man in the world, but my vagina wishes she were a greedy bitch to claim all the tongues, fingers, and dicks she fancies. Thankfully, I have a strong mind to control my ferocious need for physical pleasure.

When Karrie's on the till, I know I won't be forced into mindless conversation to fill the dead air like most cashiers feel a need to do. She's quiet as she pops her gum and scans each item before bagging them.

"Heather." Mr. Greer is behind me, wearing a big smile behind his grey beard. "How have you been and how is that husband of yours? Busy, I assume."

It's not easy keeping my eyes from drifting over his head to his handsome son, but I manage.

"I'm well. He's well, but yes, he's busy. We've been prepping our firewood for next winter. He's finishing up with the log he pulled in yesterday while I run errands." My hand brushes over his grey and black plaid jacket sleeve. "How have you been, Mr. Greer?"

A shaky hand covers mine on his arm. "Oh, for God's sake, Heather. Call me Kirk."

My head tilts as heat flushes my cheeks. "I have a hard time with that. It's a respect thing."

It doesn't go unnoticed that he's avoided answering my question of his health.

"You're the sweetest girl." He smiles but, as if suddenly aware his son is behind him, his head shakes as he steps aside to introduce the sexy-as-fuck mountain of a man. "Heather, this is my son, Dane."

There's no avoiding eye contact when his deep voice calls out to me. "It's nice to meet you… Heather."

My eyes drift down his short-bearded chin to his Adam's apple when it bobs.

"Yes. It's nice to meet you, too, Dane."

"That'll be $57.35." Karrie's gentle voice saves me from the repetitive nods I can't stop myself from doing. What the fuck is wrong with me?

After tapping my card, I put the bags in my cart and take my receipt.

"It was nice to meet you, Dane. Mr. Greer—Kirk—always a pleasure."

They mumble something, but I'm in too much of a hurry to get the hell out of there before I embarrass myself further. …

CHAPTER TWO

Dane

Heather…That's her name. How did I not notice this chestnut-haired beauty walking about the store? Only now, standing in line with my father between us, do I set eyes on this gorgeous creature.

She's tiny, very tiny. She isn't more than a shade over five-feet tall and way too thin. If she were mine, I'd feed her well to plump her up. But she isn't mine.

Dad asked about her husband. She's married. Damn. If she were single, I'd be helping her load her groceries in her car while I made small talk. After they were loaded, I'd ask her to go for lunch with me.

Heather's voice was frail, but she spoke with a sense of confidence and intelligence that intimidates me. Strong women with a gentle nature are the scariest when they're angry or feel betrayed. They may seem an unworthy opponent for a forty-two-year-old, 6'6", 250-pound man, but you'd be a fool to underestimate the evilness of a vengeful woman. I speak from personal experience.

Three months after I met Valentina, we moved in together. We married not long after that. Saying Val was a spirited woman with a temper was an understatement. I loved how she'd get herself frustrated until the yelling would start. The way she calmed down was to drop to her knees: a signal I recognized as her request for me to help her escape herself through pain and pleasure. I was always there to appease her.

She was my everything, but she was diagnosed with cancer. It devastated us.

Val fought hard. She tried so many treatments that only made her feel worse. Just over a year of medical torture—as she called it—she decided to stop all treatments. It took three months for cancer to wither her away to flesh and bone before it stole her from me.

Val passed away four years ago. She was twenty-seven years old. Something inside me died alongside her. I've never been the same.

It's been four years since she passed, and I haven't dated anyone since.

I had only one intimate experience after she died, but it didn't go well. It was only two months after I buried Val, and I was still in a state of darkness.

Did I love Val? Yes, very much. She was sweet, and I was a lucky man to have such a wonderful life partner. I regret with everything I have that I couldn't save her.

She was only 5'5" with a pear-shaped frame and trained in self-defence. She could have kicked my ass any time she wanted, and I never would have fought back. But I never gave her a reason to want to hurt me.

Fuck, I miss her!

Six months later, my golden lab, Kiddie, passed away. He was my buddy, but he was Val's guardian. After she passed, he walked around the house, searching for her at least twice a day. He missed her terribly. No matter how much love I showed him, it was Valentina he wanted.

Kiddie's name was stupid, but the two-year-old kid next door loved to play with her when she was a small pup. They were so cute together. He didn't understand the difference between cats and puppies, so he called her Kitty. Even though we corrected him multiple times, he insisted on calling her a kitty. So, it stuck. Val changed the spelling to give her some canine dignity.

She loved her daily walks on the trails. The entire time, she'd wag her tail and trade one stick for another. Each time Kiddie came across a stick or small branch, she'd drop the one she had and take the new one. Some she'd skip over. I'll never understand why dogs will pick up one stick and not the other. But she was my girl.

Kiddie loved to cuddle. Her favourite thing to do was hop in my spot in the bed when I'd get up before Val. Val would wrap her arm around the dog and go back to sleep. I have so many pictures of them in bed together. Kiddie was there for her, always.

So, I had Kiddie cremated and buried her ashes with Valentina. She can continue to comfort and protect her wherever she is now.

It all happened four years ago. Other than that one encounter, I haven't been with a woman since. I need time to figure out what I want out of life. From the time I was twenty years old and out of college, I've been working as an editor/writer at the same newspaper company. It's boring as hell, but the money and the benefits are great. Having been there for twenty-two years has earned me a prominent position with plenty of freedoms.

There are a great bunch of guys who I hang out with in Toronto when we have free time in our schedules. Some are lawyers or accountants, some are ex-bikers with rap sheets, and a few of them are fathers. A couple of them look like they'd shoot you in the head if you looked at them sideways, but they're actually a bunch of really great guys.

Every year, we trailer our bikes up north where I grew up and where my father still resides. The guys and I get on our bikes and drive the Tail of the Dragon tour. It's a beautiful trip spent bonding like men. It's a great time for us to open up and not fear judgement for doing so. I always feel refreshed when the tour ends and I'm back home in Toronto.

Dad wasn't looking well when we did our last FaceTime chat a few days ago, so the drive up was warranted. He says he's fine when I ask, but it's obvious he's lost weight, and he looks more tired than usual. He's more tight-lipped than an oyster's shell.

Since it's spring, I'm helping Dad arrange his outdoor dining set, chairs, planters, and other things to set him up for the impending summer. Now is the time to upgrade the wood pile for next winter.

The predictors have warned us to expect a brutally cold season with more snow than they've had in ten years. The last heavy winter they had up here took out power lines, blocked the highway, and snowed people into their homes—literally. Thankfully, everyone who lives up here has a generator or two to keep enough electricity flowing to charge their electronics and keep their fridges and freezers working. All the homes are heated with wood stoves or fireplaces, so lacking heat is never a concern as long as there's enough dry wood to carry them through. Spring is usually the best time for that back-breaking chore.

This year my dad has hired a company to bring his wood and stack it for him. He said he's too old to do that shit anymore and would rather pay someone else to ruin their backs and keep mine and his intact. I told him I enjoy cutting trees and splitting logs with him, but he says he doesn't want to bother me with it.

Yesterday, I cut up two fallen trees into manageable chunks and stacked them to dry for winter. The company hadn't arrived yet, and I felt like getting rid of some frustrations. The physical strain amid the silence of the forest helped bring me back to nature. The forest has a way of stealing the burdens from my soul.

Dad pays for his groceries while I watch the gorgeous Heather load her bags in her car and walk the cart to the corral. The way her hips sway and the wind tosses strands of auburn-hued dark hair around her face captivates me. She turns toward the wind as she pulls strands from her face, and her t-shirt molds to her body. Is it slightly insane how I'm jealous of the wind because it's allowed to wrap itself around her small, supple breasts? What do they look like beneath that shirt? I'll bet the wind knows, but it's known to carry secrets away.

She looks like she might be in her early thirties, but it's hard to tell since she has one of those young-looking faces. She's fit and has excellent posture as someone who studied dance at a young age. Was she a gymnast? Is she flexible and tough enough to withstand the vicious pounding I'd give her if she permitted me? But only after she's screamed through several orgasms on my tongue and fingers.

My jeans have tightened around my groin and demand I shift my erection. Has anyone noticed my tented jeans? I have to stop fantasizing about Heather before my need to grip my cock and fuck my fist until my release sets me free grows too intense.

"Hey, Dad. Want to get a soft ice cream at Becky's before we head back? I haven't had one in a while."

Dad takes out his wallet to pay for the groceries despite my argument to let me pay. His intense glare that used to terrify me as a kid still affects me today, so I respectfully back off. There's no way Dad could whoop my ass with a belt now that I'm a grown man, but his scowl brings me back to my childhood days, when respecting our elders was a lesson to adhere to. I unquestionably deserved every thwack from Dad's wide leather strap.

If my forty-two years on this planet have taught me anything, it's treating people how I want to be treated. Hopefully, when I'm old, those caring for me will be kind. If I have kids—which I can't see happening at this stage in my life—they'll grow up knowing how to treat people with kindness and compassion. From what I see, parents aren't teaching their kids the basic lessons required to get them through the day-to-day tasks while they struggle to succeed with drive and honour. I get nervous every time I see some stuck-up little twit with a shitty attitude claiming the world owes them something. I can foresee my future sitting in my shit-filled diaper while I nearly starve to death because I'm too old to care for myself. If that's the way the world is headed, I hope I don't live long enough to become dependent on one of those schmucks. …

*You can purchase **THE WIDOWED** just about anywhere by clicking the Universal Link:*

https://books2read.com/TheWidowed
https://www.goodreads.com/book/show/222517246-rule-breakers
https://www.bookbub.com/books/rule-breakers-the-widowed-by-pebbles-lacasse

ABOUT THE AUTHOR

Pebbles is an Amazon top-selling romantic erotica author of plot-driven contemporary suspense.

She loves to make readers' hearts throb and entertain their minds while leaving their bodies tingling with desire. She leans toward spinning tales of bad boys with big hearts desiring women who didn't know they had a kinky side. However, she's also known for her stories of women with hardened shells and a dominant nature, but they hold a secret yearning to be loved.

Her books and short stories often take her readers into the BDSM lifestyle while revolving around real-life issues.

There's always a happy-ever-after or happy-for-now ending because we all want life to work out in the end. Her captivating stories of romance, love, and tender moments keep her readers coming back for the next hottest story.

As someone living with Porphyria, Pebbles stays indoors to avoid UV light. It's not all bad since this allows her plenty of time to write. That's not to say she doesn't love glamping, fishing, kayaking, and swimming; she simply does it with protective clothing. Where there's a will, there's a way!

Pebbles is very family-oriented. She and her husband of 30+ years raised their children in southern Ontario, where she was born and remains to this day.

Stay in Touch and receive Updates on Pebbles' Writing by joining her newsletter:

https://bit.ly/pebbleskinkynews

FOLLOW ON SOCIAL MEDIA

Facebook

https://www.facebook.com/PebblesLacasseEroticRomanceWriter/

Facebook Group

www.facebook.com/groups/pebbleslacasseandfriendsgroup/

Newsletter sign-up

https://bit.ly/pebbleskinkynews

Website

https://www.pebbleslacasse.com

Instagram

https://www.instagram.com/pebbleslacasse/

Twitter

https://twitter.com/pebbleslacasse

Youtube

http://www.youtube.com/@pebbleslacasse7554

TikTok

https://shorturl.at/SOzO8

PLATFORMS TO REAVE REVIEWS

Books2Read

http://books2read.com/PebblesLacasse

Goodreads

http://bit.ly/Goodreads_2y5xJji

Bookbub

https://www.bookbub.com/profile/pebbles-lacasse

MORE BOOKS BY PEBBLES LACASSE

Full Novels & Series

My Wife and Master Jake
Broken Charm
Snowman's Burden

Series

Rule Breakers Standalone Series:

My Best Friend's Brother
The Widowed
The Rockstar's Bodyguard

The Complete My JoeSmith Collection Boxed Set:

Anonymity
Exposed
Nurture
Unity

The Coaching Rayna Two-Book Series:

Coaching Rayna
Bound Hearts

The Naughty Goldie Series:

Goldilocks & The Three Bear Brothers
Trifecta
Overture
Liberated

Short Stories

Little Miss Muffet
Hello, Officer
Mistress Rabbit
A Run with Charley
Carter's Mistress
Still Waters Burn Deep
Dominatrix for Hire

Anthologies

Quarantined: A Boxed Set of Pandemic Proportions
Ignited by Hope charity Anthology
Stuck on You: A Passionate Ink Anthology

To read teasers and see book cover photoshoot photos by Pebbles, visit https://www.PebblesLacasse.com

Scan for Ebook Catalogue

Scan to subscribe to Pebbles' Newsletter and receive a FREE short story gift.

SUBSCRIBE TO PEBBLES' NEWSLETTER

Sign up to receive Pebbles Lacasse's newsletter and receive a free short story to welcome you. Be among the first to read teasers from the books she's writing, learn what Pebbles does to keep her busy when she isn't writing her steamy novels, discover the captivating authors she's reading, be led to books with similar genres grouped together just for readers like you, and other crazy antics.

https://bit.ly/pebbleskinkynews

JOIN PEBBLES' TEAM

Would you like to be a valued member of my ***ARC team***? Advanced Readers receive copies of my soon-to-be published novels to read with the promise to leave reviews by the date set by Pebbles.

You'll get ***my books for FREE*** *forever as long as you leave reviews!*

Sound like a good deal?

https://forms.gle/gseo39XRubENVWjA9

www.ingramcontent.com/pod-product-compliance
Lightning Source LLC
La Vergne TN
LVHW010941110826
845149LV00013B/2704

* 9 7 8 1 9 8 9 9 7 9 6 6 2 *